Dame Wiggins
of Lee
AND HER SEVEN
WONDERFUL CATS

Illustrated by
PATIENCE BREWSTER

Thomas Y. Crowell   New York

Dame Wiggins of Lee and Her Seven Wonderful Cats
Adapted from the version by John Ruskin, published in 1885

For my grandparents

Dame Wiggins of Lee
Was a worthy old soul
As e'er threaded a needle,
Or washed in a bowl.

She held mice and rats
In such antipa-thy,
That seven fine cats
Kept Dame Wiggins of Lee.

The rats and mice scared
By this fierce whiskered crew,
The poor seven cats
Soon had nothing to do.
So, as anyone idle
She ne'er loved to see,
She sent them to school,
Did Dame Wiggins of Lee.

The Master soon wrote
That they all of them knew
How to read the word "milk"
And to spell the word "mew."
And they all washed their faces
Before they took tea—
"Were there ever such dears!"
Said Dame Wiggins of Lee.

But soon she grew tired
Of living alone,
So she sent for her cats
From school to come home.
Each rowing a wherry,
Returning, you see—
The frolic made merry
Dame Wiggins of Lee.

The Dame was quite pleased
And ran out to market—
When she came back
They were mending the carpet.

The needle each handled
As brisk as a bee—
"Well done, my good cats,"
Said Dame Wiggins of Lee.

To give them a treat,
She ran out for some rice—
When she came back,
They were skating on ice.

"I shall soon see one down,
Aye, perhaps two or three,
I'll bet half-a-crown,"
Said Dame Wiggins of Lee.

When springtime came back
They had breakfast of curds—
And were greatly afraid
Of disturbing the birds.
"If you sit, like good cats,
All the seven in a tree,
They will teach you to sing!"
Said Dame Wiggins of Lee.

So they sat in a tree,
And said, "Beautiful! Hark!"
And they listened and looked
In the clouds for the lark.

Then sang, by the fireside,
Symphonious-ly
A song without words
To Dame Wiggins of Lee.

They called the next day
On the tomtit and sparrow,
And wheeled a poor sick lamb
Home in a barrow.
"You shall all have some sprats
For your humani-ty,
My seven good cats,"
Said Dame Wiggins of Lee.

While she ran to the field,
To look for its dam,
They were warming the bed
For the poor sick lamb.
They turned up the clothes
All as neat as could be—
"I shall ne'er want a nurse,"
Said Dame Wiggins of Lee.

She wished them good night,
And went up to bed—
When, lo! in the morning,
The cats were all fled.
But soon—what a fuss!
"Where can they all be?
Here, pussy, puss, puss!"
Cried Dame Wiggins of Lee.

The Dame's heart was nigh broke,
So she sat down to weep—
When she saw them come back
Each riding a sheep.
She fondled and patted
Each purring tom-my—
"Ah! welcome, my dears,"
Said Dame Wiggins of Lee.

The Dame was unable
Her pleasure to smother,
To see the sick lamb
Jump up to its mother.
In spite of the gout
And a pain in her knee,
She went dancing about,
Did Dame Wiggins of Lee.

The Farmer soon heard
Where his sheep went astray,
And arrived at Dame's door
With his faithful dog Tray.
He knocked with his crook—
And the stranger to see,
Out of window did look
Dame Wiggins of Lee.

For their kindness he had them
All drawn by his team,
And gave them some field-mice,
And raspberry-cream.
Said he, "All my stock
You shall presently see—
For I honor the cats
Of Dame Wiggins of Lee."

He sent his maid out
For some muffins and crumpets—
And when he turned round
They were blowing of trumpets.
Said he, "I suppose
She's as deaf as can be,
Or this ne'er could be borne
By Dame Wiggins of Lee."

To show them his poultry,
He turned them all loose,
When each nimbly leaped
On the back of a goose,
Which frightened them so
That they ran to the sea,
And half drowned the poor cats
Of Dame Wiggins of Lee.

For the care of his lamb,
And their comical pranks,
He gave them a ham
And abundance of thanks.
"I wish you good day,
My fine fellows," said he.
"My compliments, pray,
To Dame Wiggins of Lee."

You see them arrived
At their Dame's welcome door.
They showed her their presents,
And all their good store.

"Now come in to supper,
And sit down with me—
All welcome once more,"
Cried Dame Wiggins of Lee.